The School Picnic

Copyright © 1987 by Good Books, Intercourse, PA 17534
International Standard Book Number: 0-934672-52-0
Library of Congress Catalog Card Number: 87-14867

Library of Congress Cataloging-in-Publication Data

Steffy, Jan, 1967–
    The school picnic.
    Summary: Twenty-eight Amish children, their
teacher, and their parents celebrate the last day of school
with a picnic.
    [1. Amish—Fiction.   2. Picnicking—Fiction.
3. Schools—Fiction] I. Bond, Denny, 1952–   ill. II. Title.
PZ7.S81737Sc 1987   [E]   87-14867
ISBN: 0-934672-52-0

The School Picnic

by Jan Steffy

Illustrated by Denny Bond

Good Books

Intercourse, Pennsylvania 17534

It is early in the morning and the sky outside is dark. All throughout the countryside gas lamps are lit. And here and there, across the fields and over the creeks, twenty-eight Amish boys and girls are waking up—some when they hear their mothers' calls from downstairs, two at the crowing of a rooster, and one by a barking dog. Several awaken just because that's the time they always get up.

But none of the children wakes up by an electric alarm clock.

Ten of the children remember to straighten the quilts on their beds. All of them step, hop and slide into their homemade clothes. The boys put on their black pants, the stretchy straps called suspenders that hold up their pants, and bright colored shirts. They take their straw hats as well.

The girls pull on dresses of blue or green, purple or pink, and black aprons. Two of the older girls, who have learned how to sew, made their dresses themselves.

All of the girls and boys, except one who cut his foot the day before, go barefoot.

By the time the sun is up, the twenty-eight children are gathered around the big tables in their kitchens, eating breakfasts of eggs and bacon, or pancakes and sausage, or cereal and muffins, but always large glasses of milk, fresh from their families' cows.

Today the children do not take lunch kettles to school. They just pick up their books and say good-bye to their Mamms and Daats, their Grossmammies and Grossdaadies, and their sisters and brothers who are either too big or too little to go to school. Three of the children wave good-bye to their Great-Uncle Jake who is visiting from Center County.

None of the twenty-eight children rides a school bus. Instead, eight of them ride scooter to their schoolhouse. The others walk, some going a mile or more through meadows with grazing cows, along winding back roads, or past fields with rows and rows of young corn. The girls meet and walk together as a group, and the boys do too. Two girls walk almost the whole way by themselves because they don't have close neighbors. One third-grade boy's shaggy brown dog follows him to school every day.

Up on Windy Hill Road a woman with smiley wrinkles around her eyes snaps shut her bag of books and says good-bye to her cat, Raisin. She is Amish too, and she wears a bright green dress and black apron like the young girls do. But she has a thin white cap, called a "covering," on her head, and shoes and stockings on her feet.

She takes the shortcut across Fisher's field this morning, since she wants to get to school before her pupils do. "Teacher" unlocks the schoolhouse door just as two fourth-grade boys, full of stories about fishing, come running into the schoolyard.

Today, instead of reading, writing, spelling and arithmetic, the wiggly, excited "scholars" sing slow songs, silly songs and fast songs. They do not use a piano or a guitar or a drum, but they do use their hands for funny motions.

Too soon they must stop to practice their poems—the older children say long ones while the small boys and girls recite short ones. Everyone manages to get through the poems except for one sixth-grade boy who missed a few days of school to help on the farm. He needs some prompting.

Poem practice ends when the shaggy brown dog barks at the parade of horse and buggies marching down the road. One by one, the families of the twenty- eight children drive into the schoolyard. Grown-ups and little brothers and sisters are everywhere.

The women and girls unpack huge picnic baskets filled with hot dogs, rolls, potato salad, chips, pretzels, cookies, pies, fresh strawberries and homemade root beer.

When the food is lined up and the fire is just right, Teacher asks one father, who is the minister, to ask a blessing on the meal. At once, the men and boys take off their straw hats. All heads bow and all eyes close as each person at the picnic gives thanks for the food.

The hungry children hurry to roast their hot dogs. Ten children carefully cook them until they're golden brown. The rest prefer them burnt and crispy, except for one hungry boy who eats his cold. The parents pile their plates with goodies and fill the warm, spring afternoon with news about their gardens and the price of hay.

When plates are empty and stomachs are full, Teacher calls everyone into the school for the Program. The students stand by the teacher's big desk to recite their poems and sing their favorite songs. The smiling parents sit in the desks, beaming at each scholar, even at the boy who forgets his lines!

Two eighth-grade girls invite everyone outside for relay games. Grossmammies and toddlers, Daats and Mamms face each other for the "Egg Drop Race."

The shaggy brown dog bumps into a girl with red hair, just as she carefully hands the spoon with the rocking raw egg to the second-grader behind her.

The scholars bat first in the baseball game. Before the fathers take their turn, two fifth-grade girls get on base and the boy with the bandage knocks a homer.

But watch out! The first man hits the ball over the fence and into the alfalfa field. A home run! Some of the mothers and lots of the children on the sidelines cheer and yell!

DENNY BOND

The scholars go up and the scholars go down. The fathers worry and the fathers work! Until one tall eighth-grade girl sends the ball just over the heads of the fathers standing ready at the fence. "12-11," shouts the scorekeeper!

The babies need naps and the cows must be milked. So the twenty-eight boys and girls say their summer good-byes to Teacher and climb into their buggies for home, full of yummy food and happy memories.

DENNY BOND